SNOW BEAR'S SURPRISE

Illustrated by Piers Harper

MACMILLAN CHILDREN'S BOOKS

One bright morning, Mum kissed
Snow Bear goodbye.
  "I'm going out now my little one, but
I'll be back soon. Look – the sun is up.
It's going to be a lovely day."

For Nicholas

First published in 2004 by Macmillan Children's Books
a division of Macmillan Publishers Limited
20 New Wharf Road, London N1 9RR
Basingstoke and Oxford
Associated companies worldwide
www.panmacmillan.com

Produced by Fernleigh Books
1A London Road, Enfield
Middlesex EN2 6BN

Text copyright © 2004 Fernleigh Books
Illustrations copyright © 2004 Piers Harper

ISBN 1 4050 4883 2

1 3 5 7 9 8 6 4 2

A CIP catalogue record for this book is available
from the British Library.

Manufactured in China.

As Snow Bear said goodbye to his mum in the shining snow, he thought how much she loved sunshine and pretty colours.

"I know, I'll give her a surprise. Something to make her smile," he said.

Then Snow Bear had an idea.

"I know! I'll decorate our den!"

First, he smoothed a path to the door and built little ice bears along it to welcome his mum home.

"These will make her smile," said Snow Bear. "But now I need something else."

So off he ran to see what he could find.

Before long, Snow Bear spied some icicles glittering outside the wolf cubs' cave.

"Wow! Can I have some of these to brighten our den?" he said. "They're a surprise for my mum."

"Of course. We can help too!" said the cubs. So they chose the biggest, shiniest icicles and took them back to the den.

Snow Bear and the cubs hung the icicles round the den and watched them gleaming in the sun.

"Mum's eyes will really sparkle when she sees these!" said Snow Bear. "But I bet I can find more decorations. Will you help me?"

"Of course!" sang the cubs.

At the bottom of an icy slope, they found Hare playing in the grass and flowers.

"These flowers are so pretty," said Hare. "They have just started peeking through the snow."

"They are perfect for Mum's surprise!" said Snow Bear. "Hare, will you help us pick a few?"

"Of course!" laughed Hare.

Back at the den, Snow Bear, Hare and the wolf cubs made a pretty carpet of flowers outside the entrance.

"Flowers make Mum so happy," said Snow Bear. "But she loves the forest too – let's go and find something from there. Follow me!" And they sped off across the snow.

Everything in the forest twinkled with frost. Reindeer stepped out from behind a tree.

"Hello, Reindeer! We're looking for something from the forest as a surprise for my mum."

"How about some frosted twigs?" said Reindeer.

"Oh yes, she'll love those!" laughed Snow Bear. "Will you help us choose some?"

"Of course," smiled Reindeer.

Back at the den, the friends quickly made a frosty canopy over the entrance.

"Lovely! But it needs one more thing," said Snow Bear.

"Look out!" shouted a voice from the sky. It was Owl.

"Snow Bear, I heard about your surprise and thought these red berries were just right!" he hooted.

"Mum's favourite colour. Thank you, Owl!" said Snow Bear.

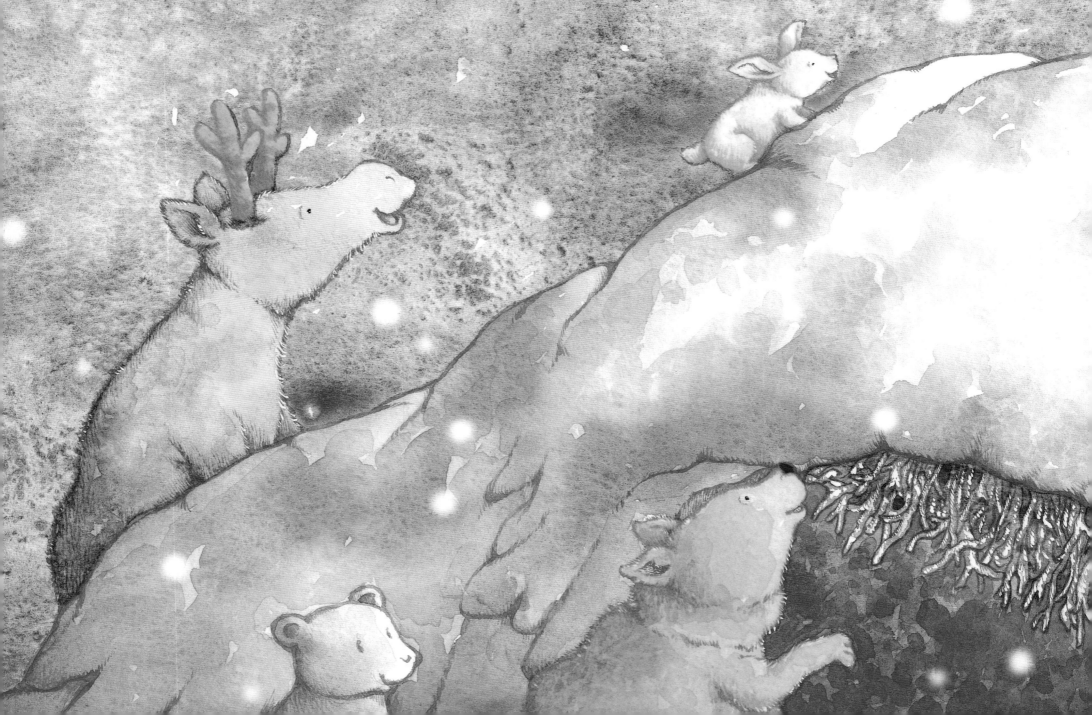

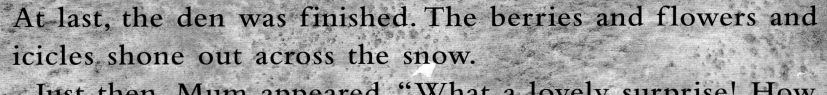

At last, the den was finished. The berries and flowers and icicles shone out across the snow.

Just then, Mum appeared. "What a lovely surprise! How clever of you all!" she laughed, and her eyes sparkled.

"Now, I have my own surprise," she said. "Are you ready for the most colourful display of all? Follow me!"

Snow Bear, the wolf cubs, Hare, Reindeer and Owl
went with Mum up, up, up to the top of a steep icy
hill. The sky was velvety dark around them, but up
ahead a strange golden light lit up the snow.

"What is it, Mum? What's the surprise?" asked Snow
Bear. But Mum just smiled.

At the top of the hill, Snow Bear gasped with delight.
The whole sky was alight with colour, dancing with
orange and yellow.

"The Northern Lights!" said Snow Bear.

"That's right, my little one," said Mum.
They all stared in wonder at the brilliant night sky.

"That was magic!" said Snow Bear later that night. "Thanks Mum!"

"But *your* surprise was the best of all," she said.

And Snow Bear and Mum snuggled closer, in their beautiful den in the snow.